THE BREMEN TOWN MUSICIANS

The BREMEN TOWN MUSICIANS

from the collection of the Brothers Grimm

Paul Galdone drew the pictures

McGraw-Hill Book Company   New York · Toronto · London · Sydney

To Boysie

There

was once an ass whose master had made him
carry sacks to the mill for many a long year,
but whose strength began at last to fail, so that
each day as it came found him less capable of work.

Then his master began to think of turning him out,

but the ass, guessing that something was in the wind that
boded him no good, ran away, taking the road to Bremen;

for there he thought he might get an engagement as town musician.

When he had gone a little way he found a hound lying
by the side of the road panting, as if he had run a long way.
"Now, Holdfast, what are you so out of breath about?"
said the ass.

"Oh dear!" said the dog, "now I am old, I get weaker
every day and can do no good in the hunt, so as my master
was going to have me killed, I have made my escape; but
now, how am I to gain a living?"

"I will tell you what," said the ass. "I am going to Bremen to become town musician. You may as well go with me and take up music too. I can play the lute, and you can beat the drum."

And the dog consented, and they walked on together.

It was not long before they came to a cat sitting in the road,
looking as dismal as three wet days.
"Now then, what is the matter with you, Old Shaver?"
said the ass.

"I should like to know who would be cheerful when his neck is in danger?" answered the cat. "Now that I am old my teeth are getting blunt, and I would rather sit by the oven

and purr than run about after mice, and my mistress wanted to drown me; so I took myself off. But good advice is scarce, and I do not know what is to become of me."

"Go with us to Bremen," said the ass, "and become
town musician. You understand serenading."
The cat thought well of the idea and went with them accordingly.

After that the three travelers passed by a yard, where a cock was perched on the gate crowing with all his might.

"Your cries are enough to pierce bone and marrow," said the ass, "what is the matter?"

"I have foretold good weather for Lady Day, so that all the shirts may be washed and dried; and now on Sunday morning

company is coming, and the mistress has told the cook that I must be made into soup, and this evening my neck is to be wrung, so that I am crowing with all my might while I can."

"You had much better go with us, Chanticleer," said the ass. "We are going to Bremen. At any rate that will be better than dying. You have a powerful voice, and when we are all performing together it will have a very good effect." So the cock consented, and they went on all four together.

But Bremen was too far off to be
reached in one day, and toward evening
they came to a wood, where they determined
to pass the night.
The ass and the dog lay down under a large tree,
the cat got up among the branches, and
the cock flew up to the top,
as that was the safest place for him.

Before he went to sleep he looked all around him to the four points of the compass, and perceived in the distance a little light shining, and he called out to his companions that there must be a house not far off, as he could see a light. So the ass said,

"We had better get up and go there, for these are uncomfortable quarters." The dog began to fancy a few bones, not quite bare, would do him good. And they all set off in the direction of the light, and it grew larger and brighter, until at last it led them to a robber's house, all lighted up.

The ass, being the biggest, went up to the window and looked in.
"Well, what do you see?" asked the dog.

"What do I see?" answered the ass. "Here is a table set out
with splendid eatables and drinkables, and robbers sitting
at it and making themselves very comfortable."

"That would just suit us," said the cock.

"Yes, indeed, I wish we were there," said the ass. Then they consulted together how it should be managed so as to get the robbers out of the house, and at last they hit on a plan.

The ass was to place his forefeet on the windowsill, the dog was to get on the ass's back, the cat on the top of the dog, and lastly the cock was to fly up and perch on the cat's head. When that was done, at a given signal they all began to perform their music.

The ass brayed,
the dog barked,
the cat mewed,
and
the cock crowed;

then they burst
through
into the room.

23

The robbers fled at the dreadful sound; they thought
it was some goblin, and fled to the wood in the utmost terror.

Then the four companions sat down to table, made free with the remains
of the meal, and feasted as if they had been hungry for a month.

And when they had finished they put out the lights, and
each sought out a sleeping place to suit his nature and habits.

The ass laid himself down outside on the dunghill,

the dog behind the door,

the cat on the hearth by the warm ashes,

and the cock settled himself in the cockloft,

and as they were all tired with their long journey they soon fell fast asleep.

When midnight drew near, and the robbers from afar saw
that no light was burning, and that everything appeared quiet,
their captain said to them that he thought that they had run
away without reason, telling one of them to go and reconnoiter.
So one of them went, and found everything quite quiet.

He went into the kitchen to strike a light, and taking the glowing fiery eyes of the cat for burning coals, he held a match to them in order to kindle it.

But the cat, not seeing the joke, flew into his face, spitting and scratching.

The robber cried out in terror, and ran to get out at the back door, but the dog, who was lying there, ran at him and bit his leg.

And as he was rushing through the yard by the dunghill the ass struck out and gave him a great kick with his hind foot;

and the cock, who had been wakened with the noise, and felt quite brisk, cried out, "Cock-a-doodle-doo!"

29

Then the robber got back as well as he could to his captain, and said, "Oh, dear! In that house there is a gruesome witch, and I felt her breath and her long nails in my face;

and by the door there stands a man who stabbed me in the leg with a knife;

and in the yard there lies a black specter, who beat me
with his wooden club. And above, upon the roof,
there sits the justice, who cried, 'Bring that rogue here!'

And so I ran away from the place as fast as I could."

From that time forward the robbers never ventured to that house, and the four Bremen town musicians found themselves so well off where they were, that there they stayed.